Transylvania
United

Written by Steve Barlow and Steve Skidmore

Illustrated by Sam Hearn

OXFORD
UNIVERSITY PRESS

In the news today, manager Abi Davis has been sacked by Downcast Rovers following a run of poor results …

ring ring – ring ring!

Hello, Abi Davis? I heard you got the sack …

Our team needs a manager.

Yeah? What about it?

Why not come over to our ground and meet the guys? I'll email you directions …

Well … OK. I'll take a look.

After all, how bad can it be?

First day of training: three weeks until the Cup Final.

We're going to start with some agility training! Sprint to the ladder, jump through it, dribble through the cones – GO!

SPRINT

QUICK STEPS

DRIBBLE

CRUNCH!

CLATTER!

THUD!

Perhaps we'll come back to the agility training ...

Let's talk tactics. We're playing Strawberry Hill Squirrels in the League on Saturday. This is what I want you to do.

POINT

We'll play 4-5-1. Stan up front. Wayne and Bob wide and linking with Vinny, Igor and Prince Toot in midfield. Any questions? Yes, Henry?

There's just one thing I don't understand, Boss.

What's that?

Everything you said after, 'This is what I want you to do.'

Saturday: League match vs. Strawberry Hill Squirrels.

Come on, you Monsters!

United vs. Squirrels

I hope they've understood what I want them to do!

phweeeeep!

Pass the ball, Henry, not your head!

Come on, you ...

Come on, you Monsters!

And the Squirrels have scored!

Oh, rats!

It was the final of the Cup, four years ago. I was playing for Downcast Rovers. The score was nil-nil. We got a penalty in the last minute. The skipper asked me to take it, so I did...

...and I sent the ball straight into Row Z!

PAF!

I never played again. I couldn't stand the thought of letting everyone down. I became the Rovers' manager instead.

A moment later...

But I'm a tactical genius! The players here don't understand my ideas. It was just the same at Downcast Rovers.

Maybe you're going about things the wrong way.

You've worked really hard, Monsters. Just go out there and enjoy yourselves.

Right, Boss!

The ref blows his whistle and we're off!

Well, look at that! The Monsters have taken Rovers by surprise and run the ball towards the goal already! Bentley passes to Zombie Stan, who runs on to it and shoots!

GOOOAAALLL!

No!

Yes!

Your tactics are working, Abi!

Wayne was right. We needed to build up their confidence. They had the skills in them the whole time!

This is UNBELIEVABLE! What a transformation from United!

If we keep playing like this we're going to win! Kev's looking pretty wound up ...

21

After extra time ...

The score is still tied at 1–1, so now we go to penalties. Each team gets three shots to see who's going to win.

Oh no — a penalty shoot-out. We've never been in one!

Don't worry, Wendy. The Monsters know what to do.

Rovers' striker Alfie Cook steps up ... and ... GOAL! 1–0 Rovers. Now it's Bentley's turn for United ... Goal! 1–1. Rovers are up again, with Slobic ... Goal! 2–1. And now it's Zombie Stan for Transylvania United, taking United's second penalty in this exciting shoot-out!

SNAP!

OOOOHHH!

Wow! It's another United transformation – quite literally!

NOOOOO!

BURST!

What a save. Now who is going to take United's last penalty? If they score, they'll win the Cup for the first time in their history.

Abi, no one wants to take our third penalty. They're all too scared of letting the team down! You'll have to choose somebody ...

I'll take it. ME!

The District Cup Final

Transylvania United vs. Downcast Rovers

£10

3pm Saturday 17th May
Wobbly Stadium

A message from the managers

Transylvania United Manager Abi Davis

I haven't been with Transylvania United for long, but I think the players here are just amazing! (Really!) They've struggled in the League, but they got through to the Cup Final through sheer grit, determination and by frightening everyone who played against them.

There can't be many teams who have a player who can ghost past a defence because he *is* a ghost. And old-fashioned wingers don't come any more old-fashioned than Skeleton Bob (deceased, 1862).

We're looking forward to meeting Downcast Rovers in the Cup Final. It'll be a game to remember (late at night when you wake up screaming)!

Come on you Monsters! Abi

Downcast Rovers Player-Manager Kevin Carter

We're looking forward to the game, which will be one of two halves. I'm sure I can count on our lads to give it a hundred and ten percent and work their socks off. There are no easy games at this level and every game is a cup final now – er, obviously.

We're a team that likes to play football. We're looking forward to lots of end-to-end stuff and goalmouth incidents, and I hope our lads will have brought their shooting boots and will find the back of the net. At the end of the day, one team will be over the moon and the other will be as sick as a parrot. It's a funny old game. Kev

The road to the final

Transylvania United	**2**
Oldtown Athletic	**1**

United defender Genni deLamp shows a new way of carrying the ball.

Swampy City	**0**
Transylvania United	**1**

Gertie Gorgon gives a new meaning to the term 'rock solid defence'.

SEMI-FINAL

Transylvania United	**0**
Chorlton Chickens	**0**
(MATCH ABANDONED)	

Chorlton Chickens players run away screaming: United go straight through to the final.

Transylvania United

Genni deLamp (full back)
Is a genie. Makes amazing things happen on and off the ball, but can be bottled up by a determined defence.

Prince Toot (centre midfield)
Egyptian mummy, recently transferred from Wadi Yawant FC (Cairo). Likes to play in a pyramid formation. In case of injury, already has his own bandages.

Frankie Stein (centre back)
A self-made man, apart from the bits that were made by (and from) other people. Takes size 19 boots. Rock solid in defence.

Wolfie Smith (goalkeeper)
Is a werewolf. He can change a game. Or change during a game. Doesn't use gloves as his hands are hairy enough not to need them.

Gertie Gorgon (centre back)
Has the hardest stare in football. Stops attackers stone dead in their tracks. Hates looking in mirrors (she finds herself petrifying).

Headless Henry (full back)
Good at carrying the ball – and his head. Once scored a goal with his head, but the ref disallowed it, saying it was the ball that needed to be in the net.

Vinny Vampire (centre midfield)
Slippery playmaker who can sail over defences and turn himself into different sorts of animals. While the other players are having their half-time oranges, don't ask what Vinny's eating.

7

9

5

11

10

6

8

Meet the players

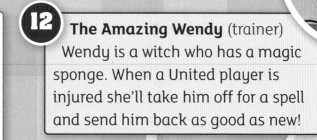

Wayne Bentley
(offensive midfield)
On loan from Grantchester City. Appears not to be dead, or able to turn into anything else. Has all his own body parts. Weird.

12 The Amazing Wendy (trainer)
Wendy is a witch who has a magic sponge. When a United player is injured she'll take him off for a spell and send him back as good as new!

13 Abi Davis (manager) After being sacked by Downcast Rovers, Abi is under pressure to prove herself.

Zombie Stan (centre forward)
Used to be called the 'Wizard of the Dribble' but now he's more of a 'Wizard with Bits Dropping Off'. Some say he's past his best since they buried him.

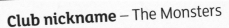

Skeleton Bob (offensive midfield)
Classy midfielder, good on the ball, but bone idle. When tackled hard he tends to go to pieces.

Igor (centre midfield)
A great servant to Transylvania United, Igor has been struck by lightning 120 times but keeps coming back for more!

Club nickname – The Monsters
Club motto – You don't have to be dead to play for us, but it helps!
Founded – 1437
Ground – Spooky Stadium
Shirt sponsors – Grimm and Reaper, funeral directors
Mascot – Coffin Charlie
Colours – Gang Green

About the authors

The Abominable Dr Barlow
and Steve 'Fangs' Skidmore
have loved horror movies since they were knee-high
to Frankenstein's mummy. They also love football.
So what could be better than a book about horror
movie characters playing football? Anyone who calls
football 'the beautiful game' has never played against
Transylvania United ...

Scarified Sam Hearn has been on the
subs' bench for Transylvania United since
about 2003. Because he can't get a game,
he's spent most of that time drawing
pictures in children's books. From cats
to meerkats, dinosaurs, people, pandas,
ghosts and pirates, Sam has drawn most
things, but this is a first for spooky monster footballers!